The Dance Fairies

For Megan, Ella and Asha Delderfield
with lots of love.

Special thanks to
Sue Mongredien

ORCHARD BOOKS
338 Euston Road, London NW1 3BH
Orchard Books Australia
Level 17/207 Kent Street, Sydney, NSW 2000
A Paperback Original

First published in 2007 by Orchard Books

© 2007 Rainbow Magic Limited.
A HIT Entertainment company. Rainbow Magic
is a trademark of Rainbow Magic Limited.
Reg. U.S. Pat. & Tm. Off. And other countries.

HiT entertainment

Cover illustrations © Georgie Ripper 2007
Inside illustrations © Orchard Books 2007

A CIP catalogue record for this book is available
from the British Library.

ISBN 978 1 84616 493 4
3 5 7 9 10 8 6 4

Printed and bound in China by Imago

Orchard Books is a division of Hachette Children's Books,
an Hachette Livre UK company

www.orchardbooks.co.uk

Tasha
the Tap Dance
Fairy

by Daisy Meadows

ORCHARD BOOKS

www.rainbowmagic.co.uk

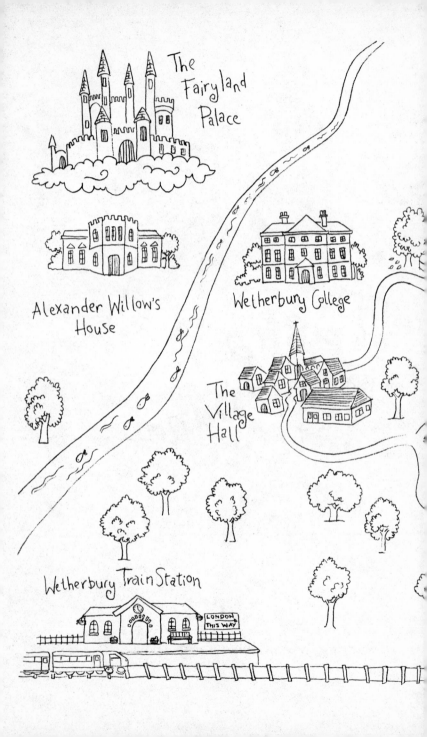

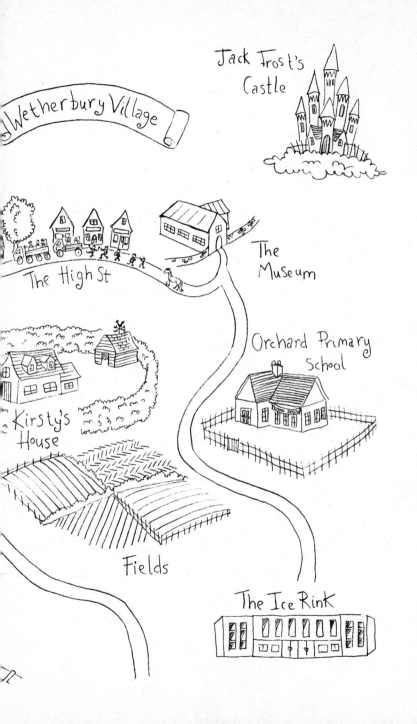

Hold tight to the ribbons, please.
You goblins now may feel a breeze.
I'm summoning a hurricane
To take the ribbons away again.

But, goblins, you'll be swept up too,
For I have work for you to do.
Guard each ribbon carefully,
By using this new power to freeze.

Contents

Tapping Trouble   9

Tasha Turns Up   21

The Big Freeze   33

Tasha's Tumble   43

Perfect Timing   53

Happy Tapping   65

Tapping Trouble

"Wow," Kirsty Tate said, as she followed her mum through the door of Wetherbury College's main hall and saw the crowds inside. "It's really busy in here!"

Her friend, Rachel Walker, who was staying with Kirsty over half-term, nodded in agreement, as she took off her

woolly hat and stuffed it in her pocket.
"There's a pottery stand," she said,
pointing it out. "Ooh, and look, they're
decorating cakes over there!"

The girls had come with Kirsty's mum
to the college Open Day. This was
a special event where people could come
and find out more about all the different

courses the college offered. Since
Mrs Tate attended a wood-carving class
at the college, she'd volunteered to help
out on the wood-carving stand and
answer any questions people might have.
All around the hall there were other
display stands showing different skills you
could learn at the college.

"There's the wood-carving stand,"
Mrs Tate said, showing the girls. "That's
where I'll be all morning, OK? But
you can wander round and look at
everything else. There's lots to see."

Rachel and Kirsty said goodbye and set
off around the hall. They
saw a man at the pottery
stand making a vase on
a potter's wheel, and
then watched as
a make-up artist
transformed
somebody into
a ghoul at the special-effects make-up
stand. It was amazing how the thick
white make-up and some fake blood
running down his chin made the
volunteer look completely different.

"Spooky," Kirsty whispered to Rachel with a shudder.

The make-up artist smiled at the girls. "You can create almost anything with the right make-up," she told them.

The 'ghoul' grinned. "It's pretty strange being turned into something else, though!" he said.

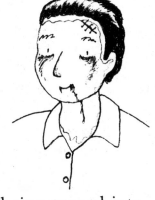

Rachel and Kirsty exchanged a smile. They knew all about being turned into *something* else. Thanks to their fairy friends, they'd been turned into fairies many times!

Only a few days earlier, Rachel and Kirsty had been plunged into another fairy adventure, this time helping the

Dance Fairies find their missing magic Dance Ribbons. So far, the girls had helped find three of the ribbons, but four others were still lost.

Just as Rachel was thinking about the Dance Fairies, Kirsty nudged her.

"Look!" she said pointing. "Tap dancers!"

Rachel turned to see. At the end of the hall, some girls in sparkly red tap shoes were practising a routine. Rachel winced as one of them clumsily dropped her black cane on another dancer's foot, and the girl next to her promptly tripped over it.

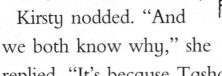

"Kirsty, did you see that?" she hissed. "The dancing is going wrong already!"

Kirsty nodded. "And we both know why," she replied. "It's because Tasha the Tap Dance Fairy's ribbon is still missing!"

The girls had learned that the Dance Fairies used their ribbons to make sure that dancing, both in Fairyland and in the human world, went as smoothly as possible. Unfortunately, Jack Frost, a bad fairy, had stolen the magic ribbons because he wanted his goblin servants to dance well at his parties.

When the Fairy King and Queen heard that the Dance Ribbons had been stolen, they went straight to Jack Frost's ice castle to get them back, but selfish Jack Frost saw them approaching and flung the ribbons into the human world, along with a goblin to guard each one.

Without their ribbons, the Dance Fairies could not work their special magic, and dancing everywhere was going horribly wrong.

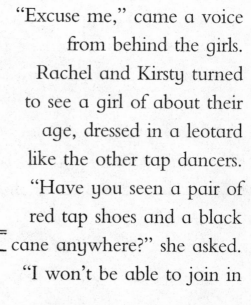

"Excuse me," came a voice from behind the girls. Rachel and Kirsty turned to see a girl of about their age, dressed in a leotard like the other tap dancers. "Have you seen a pair of red tap shoes and a black cane anywhere?" she asked. "I won't be able to join in the performance if I don't find them."

Kirsty shook her head. "Sorry, we haven't seen them," she replied.

The girl sighed. "Maybe they fell out of my bag in the car park when Mum dropped me off," she said.

"We'll go and look for them if you want," Rachel offered.

The girl's eyes brightened. "Oh, thank you," she said. "I'll carry on looking in here. I'm Ashleigh Hart, by the way."

"We're Kirsty and Rachel," Kirsty replied, smiling, as Ashleigh waved and set off to search the rest of the hall.

Kirsty and Rachel turned towards the entrance, but then stopped as they both heard a faint tapping sound which was in perfect time to the tap dancers' music. Rachel looked over at the dancers eagerly. Did this mean the magic ribbon was nearby, helping the dancers to improve?

But the dancers weren't actually dancing at all! *If they're not making the*

tapping sound, then who is? Rachel wondered.

Tap-tap-tap-tappity-TAP! Tap-tap-tap-tappity-TAP!

"I think it's coming from over here," Kirsty said, walking towards the corner of the hall.

Rachel followed. There was nothing there except a table with some leaflets on it, but the tapping definitely got louder as she and Kirsty approached. Curiously, the girls peeped underneath the table.

Tasha Turns Up

Rachel and Kirsty smiled to see a tiny fairy, with her eyes closed, tap dancing her way through an amazing routine at super-speed! It was Tasha the Tap Dance Fairy, of course! Nobody else would have been able to dance so brilliantly with the Tap Dance Ribbon missing. The fairy wore a smart-looking black waistcoat, black tights, tap shoes, and a bright red skirt.

Kirsty gave a polite cough and Tasha's eyes snapped open.

"Oh, hello," she said. "You caught me out. I just couldn't resist dancing when I heard the music."

"You're really good!" Rachel told her. "I've never seen anyone tap dance so fast before."

Tasha smiled. "Thanks," she said. "But it's a shame the other tap dancers are having problems."

She sighed. "If only my Tap Dance Ribbon were safely back on my wand where it belongs, then they wouldn't keep tripping up!"

"Have you any idea where your ribbon is?" Kirsty asked.

Tasha shook her head. "No," she said. "I haven't sensed it yet but I'm hoping it might be around here. Keep your eyes open for any goblins, girls!"

Rachel glanced nervously around. The goblins were Jack Frost's sneaky servants, and she and Kirsty had managed to outwit them in the past.

This time, though, Jack Frost had given the goblins a special power. As long as a goblin had one of the magic Dance Ribbons, he also had the power to freeze people.

Kirsty and Rachel never liked meeting the goblins, but now they felt warier than ever about tackling them. Neither girl wanted to be turned into an ice cube!

"We were just about to go outside," Kirsty told Tasha. "One of the dancers has lost her shoes and cane and we said we'd help look for them."

Tasha looked thoughtful. "Lost her shoes and cane?" she repeated.

"I wonder if they're really lost, or if somebody has pinched them!"

"Like a goblin?" Rachel suggested at once. "It's just the sort of thing a goblin would do!"

Tasha nodded, her eyes sparkling. "We'd better keep an eye out for goblins while we're looking for the shoes and cane," she said.

"Maybe we'll find the Tap Dance Ribbon too," Kirsty added hopefully. She pulled her coat pocket open. "Tasha, do you want to hop in here?"

Tasha fluttered out from under the table, her gauzy wings shimmering under the bright lights of the hall, and dived into Kirsty's pocket. "Let's go!" she said eagerly.

As the girls walked outside, Kirsty wound her scarf a little tighter around her neck, and Rachel pulled her woolly hat back on to keep her ears warm.

The college car park was directly in front of them. "Let's walk around the

edges," Kirsty suggested. "A pair of red tap shoes shouldn't be too hard to spot."

Kirsty and Rachel set off around the car park, keeping a careful eye out for the shoes and cane, as well as any cars that might be driving about. They were also half expecting to see a flash of green and a scuttling goblin, but there was no sign of any goblin mischief.

Suddenly, Tasha zoomed out of Kirsty's pocket and spun in the air excitedly, gazing out around the car park. "I can sense my ribbon!" she declared. "I'm sure it's somewhere nearby."

By now, the girls had done a full

circuit of the car park and were
back outside the main
entrance. Rachel
pointed to a path
leading around the
side of the
college. "How
about looking
down there?"
she suggested.

Tasha
nodded.
"Good idea,"
she agreed.
"My ribbon
can't be
far away."

The three friends
walked along the footpath.

They could hear the tap dance music again now, drifting out of an open window. "What was that?" Tasha whispered suddenly, hovering in the air in front of the girls. Rachel and Kirsty stopped to listen. Kirsty couldn't hear anything except the music at first, but then she heard a *tap-tap-tap-tappity-tap* in perfect time to the rhythm.

"Those are definitely tap shoes!"
Rachel said excitedly.

"And the tapping isn't coming from
inside the hall," Tasha added. "So it
must be somebody else!"

"The goblin!" Kirsty and Rachel
whispered at the same time.

The girls crept a little
further down the
path and peered
cautiously
around the
next corner.

There before them, tapping away and humming to the music, was a goblin. On his feet were sparkly red tap shoes, and in his hand was a cane with Tasha's magic ribbon attached to it.

The Big Freeze

"What does he *look* like?" Tasha muttered, stifling a laugh. "Come on," she said to Kirsty and Rachel. "Let's go and get my ribbon back!"

Kirsty, Rachel and Tasha headed over to the goblin who was far too busy dancing to notice them.

"I'll have my ribbon back now,

please," Tasha said in a firm voice.

The goblin jumped in surprise, then glared at her. "Can't you see I'm trying to dance?" he asked crossly. "I've lost my place now!" He rolled his eyes irritably, then turned away and began tapping again.

"Well, tough, because we've come to get the cane and shoes back, too," Kirsty told him. "They don't belong to you!"

The goblin stamped his foot and spun around. "You're ruining my concentration!" he screamed. "How am

I meant to dance when I keep on getting interrupted? If you must watch, please do so quietly!"

"I've had enough of this!" Tasha snapped. "It's not your ribbon to be dancing with. Give it back!"

Just then, someone must have turned the volume up in the hall, because the music suddenly got louder. The goblin launched into another routine, twirling his cane deftly in his hand as he tapped his feet.

He's good, Rachel thought, but she knew he was only dancing well because he had the magic ribbon close to him.

The Dance Ribbons were so powerful, that they could turn even the clumsiest dancer into something special if they were close enough.

The goblin seemed totally absorbed in his dancing. His eyes were screwed shut in concentration as he tapped away. Gradually, he started drifting away from the three friends and towards the music and a side door into the college.

"What's he doing?" Kirsty hissed anxiously. "Someone will see him, if he's not careful."

"I thought the goblins were supposed to be hiding," Rachel said in a low voice. "But he's not even trying."

Tasha grinned. "That's because of the ribbon," she explained. "It draws whoever has it towards music, making them dance whenever they hear a tune. Once they're dancing, they forget about everything else!"

"Well, hopefully he'll forget about us," Kirsty said, hurrying after the goblin. "And then we can grab the ribbon while he's distracted."

The girls and Tasha followed the goblin right up to the door, but as he opened it and danced through the entrance, he noticed them and stopped.

"Are you still here?" he snapped. "Well, I'm warning you, don't come any closer or I'll freeze you!"

And with that, he slipped through the door and slammed it shut, right in the girls' faces!

"Hey!" cried Kirsty indignantly. She ran to the door and turned the handle but the  door seemed to be shut tight.

"Oh, no!" she cried. "It won't open! We'll lose him!"

"It's OK, there's a window open up there," Tasha said, pointing. "I'll fly in and keep track of him."

Rachel pushed against the door with Kirsty as Tasha zipped in through the open window. "Has he locked it, do you think?" she panted.

"I don't know. Whoooa!" cried Kirsty as the door suddenly gave way.

She and Rachel tumbled inside just
in time to see Tasha waving her wand.
A stream of fairy magic whizzed
through the air and over to the Tap
Dance Ribbon, which immediately
began to unravel itself from the cane in
the goblin's hand. Rachel and Kirsty
watched excitedly as Tasha made
a dive to grab it.

But, at that same moment, the goblin leapt up and touched the fairy with one gnarly green finger. "FREEZE!" he shouted, and, to the girls' horror, Tasha instantly turned to ice.

No longer able to fly, the little fairy plummeted towards the ground like a stone.

Tasha's Tumble

As Tasha tumbled towards the floor, Rachel whipped off her woolly hat and dived forwards, holding the hat out in front of her. Fortunately, Rachel was just in time to catch Tasha softly in the hat before the frozen fairy hit the floor.

The goblin didn't seem to care. He just gave a mean cackle. "You pesky girls will be next unless you leave me alone," he told them. "So stay away!"

Then he stuck his tongue out, tightened the ribbon around his cane and danced off down the corridor.

Rachel looked down at Tasha who was still frozen rigid in the hat. The fairy's dark hair twinkled with frost, and her face had an icy blue tinge to it.

"Oh, Tasha," Rachel said, blowing on her gently to try

and warm her up. "Tasha, can you hear me?"

"How about holding her in your hands?" Kirsty suggested. "They might be warmer than the hat."

Rachel agreed and carefully scooped the frozen fairy into her cupped palm. But, at that very moment, the girls heard footsteps coming along the corridor, and before Rachel could even think about hiding Tasha, a woman appeared.

Kirsty gulped. How on earth were they going to explain away a frozen fairy?

Before she could think of anything to say, the woman began to speak.

"What a lovely ice sculpture!" she cried, peering at Tasha. "So delicate! So lifelike! I hadn't realised the college offered an ice-sculpting course as well."

Rachel could only manage a small smile in response and both girls heaved a sigh of relief as the lady smiled back and went on her way.

"Phew," Rachel said. "That was close!"

Kirsty was about to reply when a tiny, fairy-sized sneeze came from Tasha. Both girls looked down hopefully and beamed as Tasha opened her eyes, shivered, and stood up on Rachel's hand, rubbing her arms.

"Tasha! Are you all right?" Kirsty asked anxiously.

Tasha sneezed three more times, flapped her wings tentatively and then smiled. "I'm fine," she said. "Luckily, the goblins' freezing power isn't strong enough to freeze anyone for long. The magic soon wears off. And now I'm more determined than ever to get my Tap Dance Ribbon back!"

Rachel nodded. "Come on," she said. "Let's find that goblin!"

Tasha flew back into Kirsty's pocket

and the girls set off down the corridor, in the same direction that the goblin  had taken. On their way, they caught a brief glimpse of Ashleigh in one of the classrooms, still hunting for her missing things. "I hope she doesn't see you-know-who wearing her shoes," Kirsty muttered to Rachel as they went past.

They reached the hall, where the music was still playing. Kirsty looked over to where the tap dancers had been practising and gasped in amazement as she realised who was dancing merrily along with them. It was the goblin!

"Look at him!" Kirsty squealed, shocked to see him in so public a place. "I can't believe nobody else has noticed him!"

Rachel stared hard. The goblin was *very* visible, tap dancing right in front of the speakers. "Oh, and look," she said, noticing something else. "The dancers around him are doing much better now. It must be because they're near the magic ribbon!"

The girls edged closer, not sure what to do. They wanted to grab the ribbon but they didn't want to draw any more attention to the goblin.

"Look at that little green chap!" they heard a man say just then. "What a wonderful dancer!"

"He must have had his make-up done at the special-effects stand," the man's friend replied. "Is he supposed to be some kind of goblin, do you think?"

"Weird-looking, isn't he, with those great rubbery ears?" another person commented. "They can do marvellous things with make-up these days!"

Rachel had to clap her hand over her mouth to stop herself from giggling. And Kirsty, too, had to stifle a laugh.

"We've got to get him out of here," Tasha said. "It's all very well people thinking he's in costume, but what happens if someone realises that he really is a goblin?"

Kirsty nodded, looking serious again. "That would be a disaster," she agreed. "And what if Ashleigh comes back and sees him dancing with her shoes and cane?"

"I don't know," Rachel sighed, looking anxious. "He's desperate to be near the music. He's as close as he can possibly get to the speakers! How are we going to draw him away?"

Perfect Timing

Kirsty thought hard. The goblin was looking very pleased with himself. He was obviously enjoying his performance, and was even showing off to the other dancers! His cockiness gave her an idea.

"What if we persuade him to take part in a dance competition with you, Tasha?" she suggested. "I bet he won't be able to resist trying to prove that he's the better tap dancer!"

Tasha grinned. "That sounds like an excellent plan!" she agreed.

Kirsty and Rachel went over to the

goblin, and Tasha popped her head out of Kirsty's pocket. "Hey!" she called to the goblin. "You know, you're not *bad* at tap dancing, but you'll never be as good as me."

The goblin looked indignant. "*Not bad?*" he spluttered. "I'm the best tap dancer in the world!"

Tasha laughed. "No way," she replied. "I'm the Tap Dance Fairy. I'm obviously the best!"

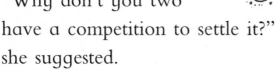

The goblin stopped
dancing and
stamped his foot.
"No, *I* am!"
he snapped.

Kirsty interrupted.
"Why don't you two
have a competition to settle it?"
she suggested.

"Yes, if you're as good as you think
you are, you should be able to follow
Tasha's steps," Rachel told the goblin.
"Or are you worried she'll be better
than you?"

"No chance!" the goblin snorted.
"OK, I'll do it and I'll win!"

Kirsty smiled. "Oh, and there's one
more thing," she added. "If you're
better than Tasha, we'll stop bothering

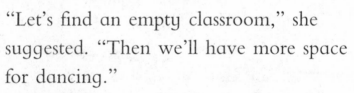
you about the Tap Dance Ribbon and
you can keep it. But if you lose, you
have to give it back."

The goblin hesitated, looking
suspiciously from Tasha to Kirsty.

"Worried I'll win, are you?"
Tasha teased.

The goblin
snorted. "As if!"
he retorted.
"Of course
you won't win.
Let's do it!"

Rachel smiled.
"Let's find an empty classroom," she
suggested. "Then we'll have more space
for dancing."

The girls, the goblin and Tasha all
left the hall and found an empty room

close by, where they could still hear the tap dance music.

Tasha hopped onto a desk. "Ready?" she asked the goblin. He nodded. "Then watch!"

She launched into a routine, tapping her tiny fairy heels and toes on the desktop, and finishing with a flourish of her cane.

"Easy," the goblin sneered, and he went on to copy her steps perfectly.

"OK," Tasha said. "Let's try another one." She tapped out a much more complicated routine.

This time the goblin simply shrugged. "No problem," he said, and copied the routine perfectly once more. "Is that the best you can do?" he smirked.

Tasha arched an eyebrow.

"I'll show you the best I can do," Tasha responded. And, with that, she threw herself into a third routine, her shoes tapping like fury on the desktop, her cane a blur as she twirled and twisted it in front of her. The goblin's mouth fell open as she finished. "Ta-dah!" Tasha cried, twirling her cane on one finger. The goblin gulped.

"Ready when you are," Rachel prompted.

The goblin shot her a glare and then began tapping. *He tried his best and he wasn't doing badly*, Kirsty thought, but the routine was just too tricky for him, and he fell over his own feet after a few moments.

Tasha smiled. "I win, I believe," she said, stretching out a hand for the ribbon.

The goblin shook his head, panting. "No," he argued. "That wasn't fair. The girls were putting me off, and…and these shoes were a bit tight, and…"

Rachel was outraged to hear so many excuses. "Tasha won the ribbon, fair and square!" she said.

Tasha gave Rachel and Kirsty a secret wink. "All right," she told the goblin. "I'll give you one last chance. I bet you can't do this!"

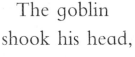

She began dancing again – and the girls could clearly see that it was a simpler routine this time. But, at the end, she tossed her cane high in the air with one hand, before catching it cleanly with the other. The fairy gave the girls a meaningful smile. *She's plotting something*, Kirsty thought, *but what?*

The goblin began to dance the routine, mimicking Tasha's steps exactly. The ribbon on the cane fluttered as he tapped his heart out.

And then, as the goblin neared the end of the routine, Rachel and Kirsty both realised what Tasha was planning.

She's hoping the goblin will toss the cane into the air, like she did, Kirsty thought. *And, if he does, maybe Rachel or I can catch it!*

Kirsty held her breath as the goblin tapped his last steps.

"Now!" Tasha shouted to the girls, as the goblin flipped the cane into the air.

Happy Tapping

Kirsty darted forward, her arm outstretched, her gaze fixed on the falling cane. The goblin realised he'd been caught out and he jumped up to try and catch the cane, too.

But Kirsty was taller and she got there first. "Got it!" she cheered, as her fingers closed around the cane.

Quickly, she detached the magic ribbon and gave it to Tasha, who shrank it down to its Fairyland size and reattached it to her wand. A flurry of sparkles and tiny top hats whirled around the wand as it met the ribbon, and the ribbon itself shimmered brightly with fairy magic.

"That's better!" Tasha beamed.

"Thanks, Kirsty!"

The goblin looked as if he couldn't quite believe what had just happened. "But…" he stuttered. "But…" He stamped his foot. "You tricked me!" he yelled.

Rachel shook her head. "Tasha won that ribbon fairly when she danced better than you," she told him. "But you wouldn't give it to her. So what choice did we have?"

The goblin glared. "Thieves! Cheats!" he fumed. "Tricksters!"

Tasha looked stern. "Jack Frost shouldn't have taken the ribbons in the first place," she reminded him.

"He's the thief, not us!"

"And you're a thief, too," Kirsty said, "stealing someone else's tap shoes and cane like that!" The goblin stuck his tongue out. "Well, you're not getting the *shoes* back," he said, glancing down at them. "I'm keeping them to dance with." And

as if to prove it, he started dancing. However, without the ribbon's magical powers, he had no sense of rhythm or balance and moments later, he tripped over and landed on his bottom.

His face flushed dark green with rage and he took off the shoes and hurled them into the corner of the room.

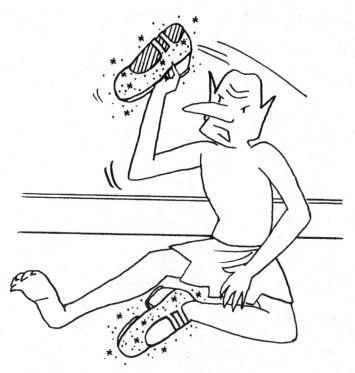

"Stupid shoes!" he muttered, then jumped to his feet and stomped off in disgust.

Tasha pointed her wand at the shoes. A stream of fairy dust and little top hats swirled from the tip of her wand and floated gently over to them. Immediately the shoes began tip-tapping their way across the floor to the girls.

Rachel laughed as she bent down and picked the tap shoes up. "Thanks, Tasha," she said.

"I should be thanking you two," Tasha replied. "You've both been wonderful, but now I must return to Fairyland! Goodbye, girls." And blowing kisses to Rachel and Kirsty, Tasha disappeared in a shower of ruby red sparkles.

Rachel and Kirsty waved goodbye and then went to look for Ashleigh.

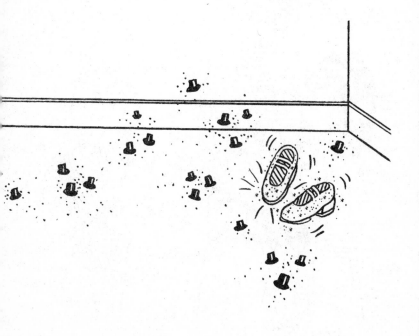

"Oh, thank you!" Ashleigh beamed, when she saw her shoes and cane. "You've saved the day! We're just about to start our show."

"You're welcome," Rachel said, smiling.

"We're looking forward to seeing you dance," Kirsty added.

Rachel and Kirsty watched as Ashleigh ran over to join the rest

of her dance class, ready for their performance. The teacher introduced the dance and turned on the music.

Rachel and Kirsty couldn't help feeling a tiny bit nervous as they watched – they'd seen so many dance performances go wrong lately! But this one went perfectly and Ashleigh's dancing was beautiful.

"And it's all because Tasha's got her ribbon back again," Kirsty said happily.

"Yes," Rachel agreed with a grin. "I love helping the fairies!"

The Dance Fairies

Tasha the Tap Dance Fairy has got her magic ribbon back. Now Rachel and Kirsty must help

Jessica the Jazz Fairy

BETHANY
THE BALLET FAIRY
978-1-84616-490-3

JADE
THE DISCO FAIRY
978-1-84616-491-0

REBECCA
THE ROCK 'N' ROLL FAIRY
978-1-84616-492-7

TASHA
THE TAP DANCE FAIRY
978-1-84616-493-4

JESSICA
THE JAZZ FAIRY
978-1-84616-495-8

SASKIA
THE SALSA FAIRY
978-1-84616-496-5

IMOGEN
THE ICE DANCE FAIRY
978-1-84616-497-2

Win Rainbow Magic goodies!

In every book in the Rainbow Magic Dance Fairies series (books 50-56) there is a hidden picture of a ribbon with a secret letter in it. Find all seven letters and re-arrange them to make a special Dance Fairies word, then send it to us. Each month we will put the entries into a draw and select one winner to receive a Rainbow Magic Sparkly T-shirt and Goody Bag!

Send your entry on a postcard to Rainbow Magic Dance Fairies Competition, Orchard Books, 338 Euston Road, London NW1 3BH. Australian readers should write to Hachette Children's Books, Level 17/207 Kent Street, Sydney, NSW 2000. New Zealand readers should write to Rainbow Magic Competition, 4 Whetu Place, Mairangi Bay, Auckland, NZ. Don't forget to include your name and address. Only one entry per child. Final draw: 30th September 2008.

Good luck!

Have you checked out the

website at:
www.rainbowmagic.co.uk

RAINBOW magic®

by Daisy Meadows

The Rainbow Fairies

Ruby the Red Fairy	ISBN	978 1 84362 016 7
Amber the Orange Fairy	ISBN	978 1 84362 017 4
Saffron the Yellow Fairy	ISBN	978 1 84362 018 1
Fern the Green Fairy	ISBN	978 1 84362 019 8
Sky the Blue Fairy	ISBN	978 1 84362 020 4
Izzy the Indigo Fairy	ISBN	978 1 84362 021 1
Heather the Violet Fairy	ISBN	978 1 84362 022 8

The Weather Fairies

Crystal the Snow Fairy	ISBN	978 1 84362 633 6
Abigail the Breeze Fairy	ISBN	978 1 84362 634 3
Pearl the Cloud Fairy	ISBN	978 1 84362 635 0
Goldie the Sunshine Fairy	ISBN	978 1 84362 636 7
Evie the Mist Fairy	ISBN	978 1 84362 637 4
Storm the Lightning Fairy	ISBN	978 1 84362 638 1
Hayley the Rain Fairy	ISBN	978 1 84362 641 1

The Party Fairies

Cherry the Cake Fairy	ISBN	978 1 84362 818 7
Melodie the Music Fairy	ISBN	978 1 84362 819 4
Grace the Glitter Fairy	ISBN	978 1 84362 820 0
Honey the Sweet Fairy	ISBN	978 1 84362 821 7
Polly the Party Fun Fairy	ISBN	978 184362 822 4
Phoebe the Fashion Fairy	ISBN	978 1 84362 823 1
Jasmine the Present Fairy	ISBN	978 1 84362 824 8

The Jewel Fairies

India the Moonstone Fairy	ISBN	978 1 84362 958 0
Scarlett the Garnet Fairy	ISBN	978 1 84362 954 2
Emily the Emerald Fairy	ISBN	978 1 84362 955 9
Chloe the Topaz Fairy	ISBN	978 1 84362 956 6
Amy the Amethyst Fairy	ISBN	978 1 84362 957 3
Sophie the Sapphire Fairy	ISBN	978 1 84362 953 5
Lucy the Diamond Fairy	ISBN	978 1 84362 959 7

The Pet Keeper Fairies

Katie the Kitten Fairy	ISBN	978 1 84616 166 7
Bella the Bunny Fairy	ISBN	978 1 84616 170 4
Georgia the Guinea Pig Fairy	ISBN	978 1 84616 168 1
Lauren the Puppy Fairy	ISBN	978 1 84616 169 8
Harriet the Hamster Fairy	ISBN	978 1 84616 167 4
Molly the Goldfish Fairy	ISBN	978 1 84616 172 8
Penny the Pony Fairy	ISBN	978 1 84616 171 1

The Fun Day Fairies

Megan the Monday Fairy	ISBN	978 184616 188 9
Tallulah the Tuesday Fairy	ISBN	978 1 84616 189 6
Willow the Wednesday Fairy	ISBN	978 1 84616 190 2
Thea the Thursday Fairy	ISBN	978 1 84616 191 9
Freya the Friday Fairy	ISBN	978 1 84616 192 6
Sienna the Saturday Fairy	ISBN	978 1 84616 193 3
Sarah the Sunday Fairy	ISBN	978 1 84616 194 0

The Petal Fairies

Tia the Tulip Fairy	ISBN	978 1 84616 457 6
Pippa the Poppy Fairy	ISBN	978 1 84616 458 3
Louise the Lily Fairy	ISBN	978 1 84616 459 0
Charlotte the Sunflower Fairy	ISBN	978 1 84616 460 6
Olivia the Orchid Fairy	ISBN	978 1 84616 461 3
Danielle the Daisy Fairy	ISBN	978 1 84616 462 0
Ella the Rose Fairy	ISBN	978 1 84616 464 4

The Dance Fairies

Bethany the Ballet Fairy	ISBN	978 1 84616 490 3
Jade the Disco Fairy	ISBN	978 1 84616 491 0
Rebecca the Rock'n'Roll Fairy	ISBN	978 1 84616 492 7
Tasha the Tap Dance Fairy	ISBN	978 1 84616 493 4
Jessica the Jazz Fairy	ISBN	978 1 84616 495 8
Saskia the Salsa Fairy	ISBN	978 1 84616 496 5
Imogen the Ice Dance Fairy	ISBN	978 1 84616 497 2

Holly the Christmas Fairy	ISBN	978 1 84362 661 9
Summer the Holiday Fairy	ISBN	978 1 84362 960 3
Stella the Star Fairy	ISBN	978 1 84362 869 9
Kylie the Carnival Fairy	ISBN	978 1 84616 175 9
Paige the Pantomime Fairy	ISBN	978 1 84616 209 1
Flora the Fancy Dress Fairy	ISBN	978 1 84616 505 4
The Rainbow Magic Treasury	ISBN	978 1 84616 047 9
Fairy Fashion Dress-Up Book	ISBN	978 1 84616 371 5
Fairy Friends Sticker Book	ISBN	978 1 84616 370 8
Fairy Stencils Sticker Colouring Book		978 1 84616 476 7
Fairy Style Fashion Sticker Book		978 1 84616 478 1

Coming soon:

Chrissie the Wish Fairy	ISBN	978 1 84616 506 1

All priced at £3.99.
Holly the Christmas Fairy, Summer the Holiday Fairy, Stella the Star Fairy,
Kylie the Carnival Fairy, Paige the Pantomime Fairy, Flora the Fancy Dress Fairy and
Chrissie the Wish Fairy are priced at £5.99. *The Rainbow Magic Treasury* is priced at £12.99.
Rainbow Magic books are available from all good bookshops, or can be ordered
direct from the publisher: Orchard Books, PO BOX 29, Douglas IM99 1BQ
Credit card orders please telephone 01624 836000
or fax 01624 837033 or visit our Internet site: www.orchardbooks.co.uk
or e-mail: bookshop@enterprise.net for details.

To order please quote title, author and ISBN and your full name and address.
Cheques and postal orders should be made payable to 'Bookpost plc.'
Postage and packing is FREE within the UK
(overseas customers should add £2.00 per book).
Prices and availability are subject to change.

Look out for the Sporty Fairies!

HELENA
THE HORSERIDING FAIRY
978-1-84616-888-8

FRANCESCA
THE FOOTBALL FAIRY
978-1-84616-889-5

ZOE
THE ROLLERBLADING FAIRY
978-1-84616-890-1

NAOMI
THE NETBALL FAIRY
978-1-84616-891-8

SAMANTHA
THE SWIMMING FAIRY
978-1-84616-892-5

ALICE
THE TENNIS FAIRY
978-1-84616-893-2

GEMMA
THE GYMNASTICS FAIRY
978-1-84616-894-9

Available
April 2008